GW00703311

# Between the Lines
## Linda Leatherbarrow

Illustrations by David Eccles

*Design by 875 Design*

First published in 2010 by
Slightly Foxed Limited
67 Dickinson Court
15 Brewhouse Yard
London ECIV 4JX

tel 020 7549 2121/2111
fax 0870 1991245
e-mail all@foxedquarterly.com
www.foxedquarterly.com

ISBN 978-1-906562-22-9

*Printed and bound by Smith Settle, Yeadon, West Yorkshire*

# Between the Lines

While enjoying an unaccustomed and leisurely breakfast in bed, Rose was struck by a new thought. She laid down her toast, flicked away a crumb, and gazed gloomily at her surroundings: whatnots, little gilt console tables and hand-me-down tapestry chairs, and that was only the bedroom. What had once seemed so comfortable, offering continuity and a well-polished notion of permanence, was now nothing more than a baleful echo. There was no getting away from it, her flat was just like the Museum. The Westgate Museum, that is, where until yesterday she had worked.

She began to off-load her furniture on to family and friends.

'Are you sure, are you really sure? How will you cope without . . . and so soon after your . . . ?'

'Not at all,' Rose replied, jumping swiftly in. 'Perfect timing.'

She didn't want to hear them say it – *retirement*; such a horrible word suggesting slippers. She didn't let on that retirement was really a euphemism for redundancy, one suggested by the Museum, not by her, but twenty-three years of beehive thimbles and decorated spindle whorls was more than enough for anybody. And besides, she drew the line at slippers.

'Are you moving?' asked her landlord, emerging from his ground-floor flat.

'Just having a clear-out, Mr Aldridge. That's all,' she said as she helped a man-with-a-van shift a heavy Victorian wardrobe through the communal hall.

Mr Aldridge raised one bristly, silver eyebrow, but Rose took no notice. She was much too busy scooping up fallen coat-hangers and hurling them into the van. Vases, ornaments, pictures, curtains, cushions – everything was given away to anyone who would take it. If she put something outside by the front gate (a broken umbrella-stand, for instance) then, in moments – *pouf* – it was gone. Nothing could have been more liberating.

Soon she had whittled her possessions down to clothes she actually wore, plus a few kitchen and bathroom necessities. And her books? Wondering if she should carry on whittling, she ran a finger along their spines: battered old Penguins, shiny new hardbacks; all of them repositories of secret explorations and discoveries; all of them granting safe conduct through past and future, seen and unseen. From *Little Red Riding Hood* to Richard Ford's *The Sportswriter* (a book she had almost not read because of its off-putting title but currently her favourite), it was books, more than anything else, that decided not just how she spoke and thought, but who she was.

No – discarding books was unthinkable. Whittling should cease.

So it was that, wrapped in her purple wool coat, she lay on a just-delivered divan drinking mug after mug of Lapsang Souchong, telling herself that this was great. These empty pea-green walls were great, this uncluttered beige carpet, this newly spacious loft-apartment (for loft read attic), this uncurtained view over Tooting Common. For three days, she did nothing but listen to the wind in the chimney and observe wild-horse clouds zipping past the palest daytime moon. She didn't even read. So many words, thousands of words already consumed every day. And in fifty-six years of reading?

From downstairs came a distant rattle at the front door, a thud that spelled *post*.

Rose found Mr Aldridge had beaten her to it; there he was, bending over the doormat in the hall. He straightened up and she noticed his eyes – puffy and red-rimmed.

'Onions,' he said, sniffing and dabbing at his face with the tip of his silk cravat. 'They always get me going,' though there was no smell of onion in the house and he was hardly dressed for cooking. In his sharp black suit with buttoned-up waistcoat and Liberty cravat, he looked as if he was just about to pop out to an exclusive club for dinner. Except for his feet, encased in tartan Doc Marten boots.

Her own sported gold lamé ballet pumps.

'Only a freebie,' he said. 'Any use?'

Rose found freebies particularly reassuring, filled as they were with advertisements for canine gyms and stories of marauding teenagers doing despicable deeds in municipal flower-beds. It was one thing to be confused by life at the beginning but quite another to be still confused later on. Back upstairs, she plunged straight in: News, Entertainment, Lifestyle, heartbreaking animal stories, all very enjoyable, but then came the small ads. She wasn't going to look at those, just as she wasn't going to check out the local second-hand shops or antique dealers. She had her redundancy money (surprisingly generous) and in due course she would go shopping, but everything she bought from now on was going to be up-to-the-minute, brand-new.

Even if the item in the far left column *was* leaping out at her, she wouldn't look. Even if it was shrieking at her like a child in dressing-up clothes on a wet afternoon.

Assorted wooden letters and printer's ornaments. £50.

Wooden letters! She pictured them standing smartly to attention in a row on her empty mantelpiece. She could make a new word every day, surprise herself with a new sentence, or even a slogan, something inspirational – *Keep Calm and Carry On*. But she didn't want to 'carry on', didn't want to be stoic and long-suffering. She wanted, as they used to say during increasingly fractious meetings at work, to 'embrace change'. Positive change that is, not – perish the thought – the sort of change that actually went on at the Museum.

Closing her eyes, she let herself fall, not to how it was before, but towards the red and green flickering patterns behind her eyelids. She wanted to be, as every self-help guru advised, 'in the moment'. She gave it one moment then wandered over to the back window. Down below, Mr Aldridge's black-and-white tom negotiated an over-long lawn, pearly with frost. After every step, he picked up each paw in turn then shook it before venturing on. Again, she thought of the Museum. There, for every laborious step forward, you had to wait weeks, months or sometimes (and this was not unusual) even years, before the final go-ahead.

*

The address given in the small ad was in Holborn, off Lincoln's Inn Fields. Tucked away behind the tennis courts, every tall dark house seemed to wear a brass plate. Rose stopped at the end of the row. Miss Ursula Panesar. She pressed the buzzer, spoke into the entry-phone.

'Come in, come in.'

Miss Panesar strode down a white corridor, polished boards below, a constellation of spotlights above. 'Excellent,' she said. 'While I do love the letters, I simply don't have the room . . .' Her black hair was scraped back and, in a little alcove, a curled white wig waited beside a briefcase. 'Well, of course, in the right hands,' she said.

Rose caught a glimpse of huge cream leather sofas, a Gilbert and George panel, a glimmer of stainless steel behind a wall of

glass bricks. Nothing older than yesterday, she thought with a first real stab of regret for all that she'd given away. Too late now. But there was something she still possessed, not an object to be dispatched, stolen or lost, but something intangible, like the lines of a poem learned at school that could only be appreciated much later; something important that would stand her in good stead. If only she could remember what it was.

'There you go,' said Miss Panesar, pointing to a large cardboard box that squatted on a cream rug, like a yogi preparing to fly. 'You have brought a car, I take it?'

'Just my cheque book,' said Rose. 'May I have a look?'

'It's all there,' snapped Miss Panesar. 'As stated in my advertisement. Look, if you don't mind, I'm rather pressed just now.' She glanced at the gold watch on her wrist, pulled a face. 'Running late for Court.'

Of course, thought Rose. Dodgy expenses claims or identity theft? Celebrity blackmail with menaces or international terrorism?

'Oh, and if it's any use,' said Miss Panesar, pointing to a lumpy shape beneath a grey plastic cover, 'you might as well take that.'

That, whatever it was, was about the size of a domestic sewing-machine.

'If you're taking the letters, you'll need it. Unless you've already got a press?'

*

'Forgotten your key?' said Mr Aldridge, one hand stroking the loose knot in his cravat – that morning he wore it low like a schoolboy, adrift on his snowy chest – while his other hand clung to the doorknob as if he wasn't sure if he should let her back in.

'I was wondering, if you wouldn't mind . . . if you could possibly give me a hand,' Rose said, still a little breathless from heaving everything out of the taxi and up the front steps.

Mr Aldridge gazed indifferently at her purchases. 'No can do.' The firmness of his words was rather undermined by the weariness of his tone. Or was it sadness? Were they heading for another 'onion' moment? 'Have to watch my back,' he added before retreating.

'Fine,' she said, to the empty porch. 'That's absolutely fine.'

She dragged the press and the box of letters into the hall and across the tiles, then bumped them up the stairs. Fancy asking Mr Aldridge for help. She hardly knew him, even though she'd lived in his house for years. Which was how she liked it; it didn't do to get chummy with your landlord. And no doubt that was how he liked it – a proper distance maintained. Did he think he had a monopoly on being miserable? There wasn't a sound except the scrape of cardboard and metal and her own muffled swearing as, head down, she hauled both items up and up. First floor, second floor, third. Then into her sitting-room with Mr Aldridge's black-and-white tom appearing suddenly and slipping in ahead of her. When she finally sat down and took stock, she was hot and dizzy, but for the first time in far too long came a sense of real attainment, a heart-skip.

Lifting the cover off the press, she saw a machine that had clearly been well looked after, no rust, no grime, but also no instruction manual, fully illustrated or otherwise. She was so hopeless with machinery – at times even the central heating dial defeated her. The box looked much more interesting, sagging and creased, and tied up with hairy string, the sort you can only buy in old-fashioned ironmongers. It took some time (she had plenty of that now) to coax the string off the box and in doing so she tore her thumb on a broken staple, but it was almost a drum-roll moment when she finally prized open the last flap and peered inside.

More boxes, and all tied with more hairy string. Sucking blood off her thumb, she lifted out a small brown box labelled 'Airfix Jet Fighter' and set it down on the carpet. The second, an unlabelled royal-blue, looked as if it ought to contain something fragrant and indulgent from Neal's Yard. The third, a gold and turquoise number, was decorated with portraits of doe-eyed ladies in ringlets, except, instead of the rustle of chocolate in little paper cases, it clunked in a way that suggested metal pieces sliding about without restraints. The fourth and last was a solid mahogany case with clip-down clasps. Now that looked promising.

But the cut was still bleeding and it hurt. Nipping into the kitchen, she turned on the tap and held her thumb beneath the stream of freezing water. There were icicles on the railings in the street below, and the sky smouldered with possible snow, just as it had last winter when she collected Laura, her little great-niece, from school. When Rose arrived, the child had jumped up and down with delight, her plump bare legs like pistons below her bright blue woollen smock. Because it's me? thought Rose, astonished, and stood, paralysed with pleasure, before finally scooping her up, kissing her, and carrying her home. Nothing had felt so good for years.

*

There was a knock on her door. Since leaving work, she preferred to keep it ajar; the small sounds of other life in the house were obscurely comforting.

'Excuse me,' said Mr Aldridge, poking his head round the door. 'You haven't seen . . . Ah, there he is. I wondered where he'd got to.'

The cat was curled up on the end of the divan, apparently fast asleep. It really was the ugliest cat Rose had ever seen. With its truncated tail and scabby flanks, it looked as if it had endured decades of war plus early-childhood trauma and desertion. It glared at both of them in turn with its solitary working eye.

'I expect he's missing Nat.'

'Nat?'

'Natalie – Miss Sedgwick. In the flat next to this one,' he said. 'You must have known Nat?'

The house, a double-fronted Edwardian villa, possessed two attics under the eaves, one on the left and one on the right, each with several rooms, originally for live-in maids.

'Afraid not.'

Mr Aldridge drew one booted tartan toe across the other, then hooked it round the back of his leg and leant against the door-frame. His mournful gaze took in the expanse of uncluttered carpet in the sitting-room, the pared-down kitchen. Rose braced herself. Was he going to be nosy or sympathetic?

'I'm sorry about before,' he said.

'That's okay. I wouldn't want you to put your back out.'

'Oh my word,' he said, his eyes lighting up. 'Is that an Adana? Yes, the old Eight-Five.' He rushed on before she could speak. 'Wonderful. Not the toy some people take it for. You'll need a proper table for that. If you'll give me a hand . . .'

There was nothing 'oniony' about him now. He pushed himself off the door-frame and padded quickly downstairs. She followed him down and into a large room on the first floor: speckled mirrors, Murano glass candlesticks, a lot of glass-fronted display cases, a huge glass chandelier.

'This should do you,' he said, sweeping a stuffed ferret in a faded ball-gown off a sturdy oak table. 'Mother's old sewing table.'

He drew out the leaves, lifted off the top and, before she had

fully taken in what was happening, Rose was staggering upstairs again, this time with her arms full of honey-coloured wood while, ahead of her, Mr Aldridge was manoeuvring a heavy frame of well-turned legs, despite his back. Five minutes later the table was reassembled in her room, the Adana perched cheerfully on top.

'Right,' he said, 'what else have you got?'

It could have felt like an intrusion but it was splendid to have somebody with her after days of being on her own and, she had to admit, the table made the room considerably cosier.

'I bought it all unseen,' she said. 'Just now, from a lawyer in Lincoln's Inn Fields, well, practically Lincoln's Inn Fields.'

'D'you mind?' he asked, then he was kneeling beside the mahogany case, unclipping its clasps and lifting the lid. He plunged his hands into the case and there, under a layer of crumpled white tissue, were the neatest little carved wooden blocks, achingly old letters that came from an age of understandable magic, when things worked because they were touchable. He hummed a few bars of *Land of Hope and Glory*, the lightest little hum, her old school song.

Did he realize he was humming?

Then she knelt down beside him and let her own hands run over the rough ink-stained wood that formed the base of each letter, the smooth polished face that formed the top. Capital F, and what was this? An M or a W? Pitted a little, some edges chipped, some letters obviously used more often than others. They were drawing them all out, examining each one and arranging them on the table, by font size, alphabetically, then by upper and lower case.

'Mostly Grotesque,' he said, 'very popular in the 1950s.'

'Look! An exclamation mark.'

He smiled, wide and toothy, a little stained by tea or tobacco, but then he was getting on a bit. But so was she, so was she. And nothing could be better, more just-right and pleasing, than that she had banished her earlier misgivings and purchased the letters. Even if they were old and second-hand.

'Ampersand,' he said, 'semicolon, dash.' He wasn't exactly jumping up and down with excitement, and neither was she, but at least he was smiling.

'Metal was my line,' he said, 'but these are beautiful.'

'Metal?'

'I used to run a little shop in Stockwell – TypeFace – perhaps you knew it? Everything you could possibly need, from Gill Sans to Baskerville.'

She hadn't imagined him in a shop, but engaged in something rather more risqué, conducted at night or behind drawn curtains.

'More interesting than you might imagine,' he said, stretching and rearranging himself, until, far from kneeling on a humble beige carpet in Tooting, he could have been standing in front of a camera. His voice became smooth, youthful, presenterly. 'The typographer's task is to erect a window between the reader inside the room and the landscape outside, conjured by the author's words.'

'Yes,' she said. 'I see.' Hence Windows XP. Except it didn't work on screen, did it? Quite the opposite. Sometimes, answering emails at the Museum or wading through spreadsheets, she'd felt like one of the exhibits, an empty suit of armour hacking at an alien bombardment with a rusty sword. Not any more, she thought. Not any more. But there was a definite pang. For her colleagues? For being needed each and every day? For spreadsheets and budget controls? Forget it, she thought. That was then and this is now.

'Typography works with the unconscious mind,' he said.

'The inner eye focuses *through* it and not *upon* it. Good type is transparent; it never intrudes or imposes. Our unconscious is always watching out for mistakes, such as inappropriate setting or insufficient space between the lines. It gets easily bored or tired of immoderation.'

She picked up another letter. Immoderation, she thought. Effusiveness. Passion. It wasn't boredom that had made her throw away her belongings but a strangely righteous passion – fury. They were very close, his face only inches away. He had wonderful slate-grey eyes full of distant horizons, the world travelled, the world yet to come.

'Please forgive me, Rose – it is Rose, isn't it? You don't mind me using your first name? I was quoting from an old catalogue, a dreadful indulgence.'

His hair fell across the back of his neck in a soft silver pony-tail, fastened with a red elastic band that matched his tartan boots.

She should ask for *his* first name.

'I see you've hurt your thumb,' he said. 'Not badly, I hope?'

'No, not at all.' The note of sympathy in his voice brought a sting of unexpected tears to her eyes – but for what? Too much uncluttered space? Too much kindness? She'd forgotten about her thumb. It was bad enough, him being pink around the rims, without her following suit.

'I don't suppose,' she said, drawing the cuff of her sleeve over the cut, 'I mean, not much call these days . . .'

'Exactly.' He put out his hand, let it hover, as if he couldn't decide whether to lay it lightly on her arm or her cheek, then, faraway, the front door knocker crashed. 'Oh God! Nat – Miss Sedgwick – I forgot.' Scrambling up off his knees, he seized the cat and was gone.

Rose listened to him bounding down the stairs, a squawk that was probably the cat, then muffled voices in the hall, a door shutting, silence. Her empty green walls pressed closer. What could be so urgent?

She looked at the letter lying in her hand, but it wasn't a letter; it was a block the same size as the others but this time topped with a copper plate engraved with a bird – a peacock? No, a lyre bird with a magnificent curving tail. She held it out to catch the light and her thumb began to bleed again. I should have been someone who makes things, she thought, not someone who looks after things other people have made.

It didn't do to dwell.

Plasters, bread, cheese, fruit. Time you went shopping.

But as she went down the stairs two minutes later and crossed the hall to the front door, she caught herself lingering, breathing in Miss Sedgwick's perfume (heavy on the jasmine, not one she recognized), and eyeing the parka slung over the banister post, the tatty trim of artificial fur on its hood. None of my business, she told herself. None of my business. All the same, she stayed where she was. She hung in the mirror, so much history stamped on her face: a scattering of boyfriends and two husbands blown away on the years; a roomful of friends who felt sorry for her; a niece who felt sorry for her and a great-niece who didn't. A great-niece who loved her, who was going to have a sixth birthday soon, who deserved a present and a card, who had recently learnt to read. Thank you, Miss Panesar. Paper, ink, white spirit . . .

Mr Aldridge's door sprang open and a scrawny young woman with ferociously white teeth flounced into the hall. Despite the running togs and trainers, it was obviously anger, not effort, that flushed her face. 'No way,' she shouted. 'Never in a million years!' Then she snatched up her coat and slammed through the front door, leaving Rose flattened against the wall.

'Such cheap theatricals,' murmured Mr Aldridge, materializing among the musty coats and forgotten scarves on the opposite wall.

'Mr Aldridge,' said Rose, stepping nervously forward; she hated scenes. 'I wonder, could you possibly direct me to the nearest artist's supply shop?'

His eyes passed right through her. He shook himself like a dog coming out of a canal so that she stood there in a storm of flying drops, mud, weed, dead fish, supermarket trolleys, car seats, corpses. There was nowhere for her to go, and then it all stopped. The hall was itself again; Mr Aldridge was himself again.

'Mr Aldridge?'

He held up his hand and she noticed he was no longer wearing his Liberty cravat.

'Tooting Broadway,' he said.

*

Two hours later, Rose staggered back weighed down with carrier bags, her thumb wrapped in breathable plaster. She dumped the lot on the table: a ream of creamy paper, several reams of coloured paper, a bottle of white spirit and a tube of black ink, plus samosas, pakoras, bhajis, chapattis, bright green pistachio cakes, and a silver foil container of lentil dhal. It was beautifully warm in the flat. Almost tropical. She took off her coat then, sitting cross-legged on the carpet, ate and ate and ate. It was all delicious and it was ages since she'd shopped anywhere except Sainsbury's, drifting in on her way back from the Museum, too tired to be hungry. She mopped up the last of the dhal with a corner of the last chapatti, then a two-syllable word, wreathed with garlic and spices, stepped gently into her mouth.

'Happy,' she said. Such a nebulous concept, elusive and double-edged, yet sought after like the Holy Grail. She stared at her books, shelved on either side of the mantelpiece. Those used to make her happy but, if she took them down now and turned the pages, how would they look? Were they full of mistakes – inappropriate setting, insufficiently spaced lines? She couldn't remember a single thing about their typography. The covers, yes. The illustrations, yes. The story, mostly. The typography a total blank. Was that how it should be?

Then she remembered a bookshop in Blackheath, its deeply pleasurable smell like fresh pencil shavings or, yes, Lapsang Souchong, delicate and powerful at the same time. The shelves were filled with private press editions, all new to her. Books with big bold letters on their title pages, letters that could have been printed from wooden blocks just like hers. Books signed and numbered, some bound in olive green leather, some in red linen, some printed on full vellum, some blocked in gold leaf on the front and spine, some with hand-printed Japanese endpapers and slip cases. Heavy volumes, slim volumes, pamphlets sewn together with fine silk stitches. It was as if she were at a party where all the other guests rushed up to her, held out their hands and smilingly introduced themselves – all at once.

She walked over to the table and began to move the wooden letters around. They seemed to draw together without her taking charge and that felt right; large coupled with small, fat with thin, curved with straight, those with a diagonal stress next to those with an upright stress, a full stop next to the lyre bird. Five or six letters together with one ornament made a satisfying block, any more and it got over-complicated. These letters weren't about making windows. These letters weren't transparent; they were about themselves.

*

On Saturday the front door slammed again, and on Sunday. On

Monday there was more shouting in the hall.

'You'll be hearing from my solicitor,' yelled Miss Sedgwick before slamming the door, again.

Five minutes later, Rose heard a soft little knock at her door.

'You haven't got a cup of tea, have you?'

'Only Lapsang.'

'Heaven,' sighed Mr Aldridge, plonking himself down on her divan. 'I knew you weren't a Typhoo person.'

He was wearing a pale lemon cardigan over an ice-blue shirt, and a spotted bow tie squinted under his chin. His eyes were still distinctly pink.

Rose turned on the kettle. 'May I ask . . . Is everything all right?'

He heaved a theatrical sigh. 'Nat – Miss Sedgwick – only wants my Izzy, thinks she's entitled. He went missing, for five months. Can you imagine what I was going through? FIVE MONTHS. She had him up here all that time, in her flat, and I didn't even catch a glimpse, not a whisker. I never normally come up here, her territory, well, yours too, of course. I asked if she'd seen him and she seemed genuinely sympathetic. It never occurred . . .'

'You mean he was kidnapped and held prisoner in his own home?'

'Got it in one. When I confronted her, she said she was providing him with a refuge, said he'd escaped. As if.' He heaved another sigh. 'Said I wasn't giving him enough "quality time". He's a cat! Do you know what she bought him?'

Rose shook her head.

'A fantasy fish bowl, a kitty babble-ball that says, "Chirp, chirp, chirp". Oh, and a remote-control mouse. He's got real mice in the cellar. I shut him in there sometimes – only for a few hours at a time. He loves it, but Nat thought I was being cruel.

To him, you understand, not the mice. Then he vanished. I was out day and night, checking the police, the Cats Protection League, the RSPCA, putting notices up on all the trees. I knocked on every door in the street. I even rang the Council to see if the bin men had picked him up.' Here his voice broke. Rose made him a mug of tea and he held it out for sugar before going on. 'Two spoons, please. You probably wouldn't know, but if they pick up any . . .' He took a sip of his tea. 'Lovely, thank you. Well, they keep them in their freezer for a month. And now she's threatening me with the law.'

'To get him back?'

'Yes, only now he's scarpered. Over the back wall. Probably cosying up to someone else already. I could strangle him. We go back a long way. Seventeen years thrown aside for a few tawdry knick-knacks.'

'Izzy?' she asked.

'Isambard Kingdom Brunel. I told her to leave as soon as I realized, but then she smuggled him out in the removal van. I had to ring round, find the removal company, get them to give me her address, tell them she'd left something behind, then go over there when she was at work and steal him back.'

'You burgled her new place?'

'Her landlady let me in.'

Rose made herself a mug of tea and sat down on the divan next to him. She wasn't even going to ask what story he'd told the landlady.

'I don't see', she said, 'that there can possibly be any kind of legal case.'

'You don't?'

'Go and get some sardines, some boneless kipper fillets, whatever he likes best, and put them out on the back wall, then *you'll* have to keep him in for a bit. Not answer the front door until

Miss Sedgwick calms down.' It didn't seem appropriate to use her first name – a woman who could stoop so low.

Leaning forward, he gave her a quick peck on the cheek. 'Thanks,' he said. 'I feel so much better now. Justin, please. Call me Justin. Of course you're right. That's what I'll do. I imagined Izzy running all the way back to Battersea.'

'Is that where *she* lives now?'

'Near the park.'

They sat quietly on the divan together until they had drunk their tea.

'Have you had a go?' he asked, nodding at the Adana on the table.

She'd almost forgotten the Adana, but now she looked again, she saw that with its robust red sides and base, its slim levers and shiny silver knobs, it wasn't just purposeful, it was beautiful. There was a flat silver disc that spun round and round and a sturdy handle that propelled a double roller across the disc – presumably that was where it picked up the ink.

'I'm not quite sure how . . .'

'I'll give you a hand,' he said. 'It will be a pleasure. But first, the fish shop.'

Standing at her front window, she waited to see him go down the street, his shoulders hunched against the cold, his breath puffing out in front of him, white as ectoplasm. She stood there until he was out of sight, then walked over to the table and glanced down at the wooden letters.

The arrangement she had made that morning spelled HAPPY with the P's pointing backwards. She hoped they were P's. They could, of course, be upside-down d's. She wasn't at all sure about the word any more. Mr Aldridge certainly wasn't happy and she couldn't claim she was, either. Perhaps if you tried to do something interesting every day . . . perhaps if you let being 'happy' look after itself . . . Then there was her little great-niece jumping up and down, her face radiant, her arms outstretched. Five letters and one ornament in a square block that looked as abstract as a Braque, or as audacious as a Maggi Hambling, covered as it was in little marks, old ink stains, scratchings, nicks and grooves – HAPPY.

She went through her boxes again. Where were the other ornaments? So far there was only the lyre bird. The ad definitely said ornaments – plural. But the chocolate box contained nothing more interesting than narrow strips of blank metal and wood and a mallet that looked as if it should be used for tenderizing steak, the Neal's Yard box only a sad collection of dried-up tubes of ink and a palette knife, while the Airfix Jet Fighter turned out to be a green felt roll of tiny chisels (rather special these and very sharp, though not what was needed just now – wood-engraving tools?). What *was* needed was some kind of frame to keep the letters in place. The words 'printer's bed' came to mind. She thought of the printing presses in the basement at the Museum, huge steam-powered machines. What was it Mr Aldridge – Justin – had said about the Adana? 'Not the toy some people take it for.' The Museum didn't go in for toys.

It occurred to her then that there might have been another box, one that Miss Panesar had overlooked, a box full of mysterious but vital metal parts. Miss Panesar could be consigning an eight-by-five metal frame to a dustbin. The dustbin lorry could already be on its way.

*

Lincoln's Inn Fields rang with the sound of tennis balls being thwacked across nets. Young men ran around in shorts even though the temperature was barely above zero. A sparrow fluttered in front of Rose then darted on to a window-ledge. Once again she pressed the buzzer and announced herself to the entry-phone.

'I'm glad you called,' said Miss Panesar. The white wig was in its place in the alcove but, next to it, instead of the briefcase, sat a Huntley & Palmer biscuit tin. 'Meant to give it to you the other day. Bit distracted,' she said, handing it over. 'The ornaments are inside, wrapped in my uncle's work-coat – he used to wear it when he was printing. I inherited some of his stuff when he died.'

Already they were walking back down the corridor, then Miss Panesar opened the front door and looked along the street as if she'd never seen it before.

'I think that's everything now.'

'Thank you,' murmured Rose. She hesitated on the doorstep. There *was* something else but how could she possibly broach the subject of Mr Aldridge – Justin's – cat when Miss Panesar might be needed in Court. That wig meant business. Who knew what crimes awaited? There could be rape or murder in the offing. What was a kidnapped cat beside all that?

*

Justin – she really mustn't call him Mr Aldridge any more – lent over the Adana with a can of WD-40 in his hand. He was humming again, just a bar or two. He moved a lever, tightened a screw.

'The gripper fingers hold the paper,' he said. 'You can vary their length, so. The chase holds the letters and drops in here.'

'I see,' she said, hoping she did.

He put down the WD-40 and gently settled the metal frame – the chase – round her arrangement of wooden letters, then shuffled through the little pieces of wood and metal. 'Pack them round, tighten them up with the quoin. This is the quoin key.

Here, I'll show you.' He packed the pieces of wood between the letters and the sides of the chase, dropped in the quoin and turned the key until the quoin opened and made a perfect wedge securing everything snugly together.

'Simple,' he said.

Rose waited for him to say something else, but he didn't.

'Yes,' she said, unexpectedly forlorn. 'Simple.'

And then because he'd been so very helpful, she wanted to be helpful back. That was all it was really. 'I spoke to the lawyer,' she found herself saying, 'the one who sold me the Adana. Spoke to her about Izzy and your rights and Miss Sedgwick and her rights, and she doesn't have any, none at all, not a proverbial leg to stand on.'

'You did?' Justin said.

It wasn't really lying, was it? She'd almost spoken to Miss Panesar, hadn't she? She hated lying, was normally useless at it, but he obviously believed her.

'The law is on your side,' she said. 'Lincoln's Inn Fields. The very best advice. A top barrister.' She was overdoing it now, but he didn't seem to notice. He was beaming. Immoderation, she thought. Excess.

'You asked your lawyer about Izzy?'

'Not strictly *my* lawyer, but definitely a lawyer.' And then she had her inspiration. 'I take it that Izzy is chipped?'

'Chipped?'

'Yes, with his ID number. Proof of possession, that's what Miss Panesar said.'

But Justin was staring at her wildly.

'He doesn't even wear a collar. He *did*, a magnetic collar for his cat flap with a proper name-plate, but he was picking up stray bits of metal – rusty nails, dropped cutlery – clanking round the house. Nat – Miss Sedgwick – caught him in the hall, dragging a cheese grater across the tiles. She threw the collar away. Said it was causing him distress. When I got him, you see . . . well, chipping wasn't an option. Not even a gleam in a vet's mercenary eye.'

'Go and ring the vet,' said Rose, 'and make an appointment, then come back and give me a hand. Please, if you wouldn't mind. I have to make a birthday present with the letters.'

He went off to telephone and she put on the work-coat. Miss Panesar's uncle must have been a small man because it fitted surprisingly well, the sleeves just a little bit long. At the Museum it was always high heels and a straight skirt, a tidy blouse with a suitably antique necklace, her blue Egyptian beads or her grandmother's carnelians. The coat was suitably practical, made of thick brown cotton, stained here and there with inky blobs and streaks. Hands on, she thought, rolling up the sleeves. Very hands on. Then there was Justin, back already and carrying a brown paper bag.

'Three-thirty tomorrow afternoon. *This* afternoon I'm all yours.'

'And Izzy?'

'Safely shut in and fast asleep. I thought you might like these.' Inside the bag lay five unused tubes of printer's ink – red, blue, yellow, green, violet – and a small hand-roller. 'The roller's for spreading the ink on the platen, getting it to the right consistency before you operate the double roller. Are you planning on making a poster?'

'Book,' she said. 'I'm going to make a book.'

'With just these letters?'

'And the ornaments. Besides the lyre bird, I've a pair of church bells, a violin, feather pen, ribbon tied up in a bow . . . and a holly wreath.'

'Well, in that case,' he said, 'I've a cabinet downstairs with some bits and pieces from the shop. Well, more than one cabinet, actually. Very neatly made, birch-ply drawers specially designed for type. Seventy-two division wooden cases. Some of my favourite fonts. Eric Gill's Perpetua, for example, cut during the 1920s. Or French Old Style, a very good legible face, nice tapering tails on the R and K.'

'You're very kind,' she said, and truly meant it.

'Mother always said I should be a teacher,' he said. 'Couldn't have been more wrong.'

'What was she like?'

'She was . . . she was *difficult*. Not a kind person. I try not to pass that on. You have to, don't you? Try not to, I mean.'

'Yes,' said Rose and swithered then, but only for a moment. Her hand glided over the smooth wooden letters waiting on the table. 'I want to make something just with these. One word on each page.'

'So the whole book makes one sentence?'

'No, the same word on every page.'

'And the word is?'

'You'll see.'

He left her to it then. 'A little wrung out,' he said. 'I know it's pathetic, but this whole business, the thought of losing Izzy . . . silly to get so attached to an animal, especially a heartless little opportunist with one eye always on the tin-opener. Think I'll go and lie down. Can you manage now?'

'Absolutely.' Why did she say that? A word she never used, the most overused and devalued word in the English language.

'Leave you to it then. Enjoy.'

And why did he have to say that? 'Enjoy', like a waiter hovering above a feast.

It was a feast though, wasn't it?

*

27

All afternoon, all evening, and all through the night, Rose worked with the Adana and the wooden letters. It took an hour or so to get the hang of everything and then she was off – different arrangements of the same letters, different ornaments, different ink colours, different papers. Capitals and lower case. Upside down or right way up. Sideways. Wide or thin spacing between letters. No spacing at all. With each change of colour she had to clean the ink disc, the rollers and the letters. She had to cut up a T-shirt to make cleaning rags. When each page was perfectly aligned and balanced, she printed fifty sheets, just to make sure she had the very best print and because, once the chase was in place, the ink smooth and silky, it would have been crazy not to. She was enjoying herself too much to stop and besides, with only the divan and table to get in the way, she could lay out the sheets to dry across the carpet. Seven rows, seven arrangements, seven years of her niece's life, six already lived and the new one to come.

It was as if making the word physically real had made it possible again, *really* possible. Even if happiness was always transitory, that was natural and the way it had to be. She was ready now to take up all the things she'd thrown away (not literally; her old possessions were gone forever), to rediscover the other things and start again, to move backwards in time towards a different kind of newness, a wiser, older kind. Was that what she'd brought with her when she'd moved? The important intangible thing she couldn't remember? And so she went on, until there was no more floor space and the sky turned pink.

Hours later, when Justin tapped at her door, there was no answer, only a powerful smell of ink and turpentine. What if she'd been overcome by fumes? When he peeped inside, there she was, fast asleep, snoring gently, her back against the wall beside the table, no way of getting from the table to the bed, or from the door to the table without treading on inky pages. He picked up a page, touched it with the tip of his finger to check if the ink was dry, then set it back down again.

'Beautiful,' he murmured. 'Oh my.'

Then he went downstairs again, sat with Izzy on his lap, and waited.

*

So it was that later that afternoon, Rose found herself in a taxi heading back from the vet's with her landlord and a one-eyed black-and-white tom called Isambard Kingdom Brunel, a tom whose breath stank of Heritage fish paste, who glared at her balefully and kept its ears – or what was left of them – flattened against its miserable little head, a cat whose left flank was the bearer of a brand-new chip. So it was that Miss Sedgwick received a letter knocked up on a brand-new computer in Tooting's newly refurbished library, a letter couched in the very best, the most formal, Museum legalese, using words such as 'acquisition' and 'impeccable provenance' and 'clear ownership rights' and was duly scared into relinquishing all claims. So it was that, from that day on, Isambard Kingdom Brunel stayed happily downstairs, sleeping mostly (he was a very old cat) on the spots where the hot-water pipes or the morning sun warmed the floorboards, and Justin began to venture upstairs on a more regular basis. And so it was that a new private press came into being and Rose's great-niece received a first-edition book for her sixth birthday, one with a hand-printed cover and hand-printed pages, numbered and signed by her great-aunt, in which every page was a wish and every page made her smile – Happy Happy Happy.

*About the author*

Many years ago, at art school, Linda Leatherbarrow's fellow
students were producing larger and larger paintings, exuberant
and expressionist, while her own kept stubbornly shrinking.
Words began to creep in underneath or round the edges of
little prints – lino cuts, woodcuts – single words and then
whole sentences until, thankfully, they took over altogether.
*Between the Lines* is her longest short story.

Her short stories have been widely published in anthologies,
magazines (literary and commercial) and in her collection
*Essential Kit.* They have also been broadcast on the radio. In
2009 she won the Guardian Hay-on-Wye Short Story Prize.
She has also won a Bridport Prize, an Asham Award and an
Arts Council Award, and is three times winner of the London
Short Story Competition.